Inspector Flytrap

Didi Dodo
FUTURE SPY

DJ Funkyfoot

By **TOM ANGLEBERGER**

With story consultation by Oscar Angleberger

Illustrated by

HEATHER FOX

DJ Funkyfoot

Give Cheese a Chance

Amulet Books • New York

PUBLISHER'S NOTE: This is a work of fiction. Names, characters, places, and incidents are either the product of the author's imagination or used fictitiously, and any resemblance to actual persons, living or dead, business establishments, events, or locales is entirely coincidental.

Library of Congress Control Number for the hardcover edition: 2021010647

Paperback ISBN 978-1-4197-4731-1

Text © 2021 Tom Angleberger
Illustrations © 2021 Heather Fox
Chapter text excerpted from *DJ Funkyfoot: The Show Must Go Oink*
    (DJ Funkyfoot #3) © 2022 Tom Angleberger
Book design by Heather Kelly

Published in paperback in 2022 by Amulet Books, an imprint of ABRAMS. Originally published in hardcover by Amulet Books in 2021. All rights reserved. No portion of this book may be reproduced, stored in a retrieval system, or transmitted in any form or by any means, mechanical, electronic, photocopying, recording, or otherwise, without written permission from the publisher.

Printed and bound in U.S.A.
10 9 8 7 6 5 4 3 2 1

Amulet Books are available at special discounts when purchased in quantity for premiums and promotions as well as fundraising or educational use. Special editions can also be created to specification. For details, contact specialsales@abramsbooks.com or the address below.

Amulet Books® is a registered trademark of Harry N. Abrams, Inc.

ABRAMS The Art of Books
195 Broadway, New York, NY 10007
abramsbooks.com

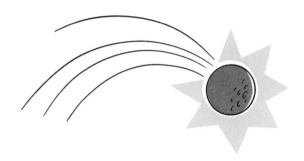

To Steve Altis,
famed miniature golfer —T. A.

CONTENTS

Opening

My phone rang.

"Greetings," I said. "I am DJ Funkyfoot, and I am at YOUR service."

"Oh, I'm sorry, sir," said a polite voice. "I was trying to reach MC Funkyfoot."

"That is also me, sir," I said, and I also spoke with a polite voice because I'm a butler and that is how butlers talk. We also say "sir" a lot. Or sometimes "ma'am" or "m'lady." Or, if they prefer, "Your Excellency" or "Your Royal Highness."

"Your name is DJ Funkyfoot AND MC Funkyfoot?" asked the polite voice. "Sir, are you a hip-hop star who is a DJ AND a rapper?"

"I am none of those things, sir. DJ is my first name and MC is my middle name."

"Your parents named you DJ MC Funkyfoot?"

"Yes," I said, still politely. "They knew they wanted me to be a hip-hop star, but they couldn't decide if I should be a deejay, who spins records to make funky beats, or an emcee, who raps words to those beats to make a cool rhyme."

"If you don't mind me asking, sir," said the polite voice, "which are you?"

"Neither, sir," I said. "I'm a butler, sir."

"Well, that is good, sir," said the polite voice. "Because I need to hire a butler, sir."

PART 1

Serving USA

Chapter 1

I was very happy to hear that someone wanted to hire a butler!

Ever since I lost my job with Countess Zuzu Poodle-oo, I have had a hard time finding a new job as a butler.

In fact, there are so few butler jobs that I could not be picky. I was ready to work for ANYBODY!

The polite voice continued . . .

"My name is Cedric Dragonsmasher, sir."

"Oh, are you a dragon fighter, sir?" I asked.

"No, that's just my name, sir."

I hate it when people ask me about my name, so I decided not to ask Cedric Dragonsmasher about his.

Instead I thought about how many times he had said "sir" in the last two minutes.

"Are you a butler, too, sir?" I asked.

"Yes, sir," Cedric Dragonsmasher said. "I work for President Horse G. Horse. I am the White House butler."

"WOW!" I almost shouted, then I remembered that butlers don't shout "WOW!"

"Very good, sir," I said calmly.

"Listen, DJ MC Funkyfoot," he said,

"since we're both butlers, how about if we stop saying 'sir' over and over? Otherwise we might be on  the phone all day, and I need your help in a hurry."

"OK," I said. "Please tell me how I can be of service, dude."

"I'm taking the day off to play miniature golf," he said. "I need you to go to the White House and be the president's butler for the day."

"Since we're both butlers and we're not saying 'sir,' would it be OK if I shouted 'WOW!'?" I asked.

"Just this once."

"WOW!"

Chapter 2

could hardly believe I was going to be the butler for the President of the United States! That's almost as good as being butler to the Queen of Wingland!

I put on my very best butler suit and my very best butler shoes and my very best butler hat.

I practiced saying "Very good, sir" and "Yes, Mr. President" and "More tea, President Horse?"

Then I called my mom. I was sure she would be impressed that I would be serving tea to the President of the United States!

"President Who?" asked my mom.

"President Horse!" I said.

"Oh, that guy," she said. "Well, maybe you can make a rap about it. What rhymes with 'horse'?"

"Gee, Mom, I thought you'd finally be proud of me."

"Of course," she said.

"You mean 'of course you're proud of me'?" I asked.

"No, DJ, I mean 'of course' rhymes with 'horse'! Now, what rhymes with 'pres-i-dent'?"

"I'm sorry, Mom, but I don't have time for rhymes, I have to get to work . . . at the White House!"

"Say hi to the res-i-dent for me!"

Chapter 3

After I hung up, I stepped outside to hail a taxi.

But before a taxi came by, a really really long limo did.

The really really long limo screeched to a stop. The driver's window rolled down.

"Hey! DJ Funkyfoot! Need a ride?"

It was my old boss, Countess Zuzu Poodle-oo. Ever since she lost all her money by investing in a giant robot, she had been driving a taxi to make a living.

"Yes, Countess," I said. "But I thought you were driving a taxi."

"Naw, they fired me just for wrecking twenty-seven taxis. So now I have a job working for the White House. I'm President Horse's limo driver!"

"That's amazing!" I said, then remembered that butlers aren't supposed to be amazed. "I am working for the president, too," I said. "For today only, I am his butler."

"I know," she said. "That's why I drove over here to pick you up. Now get in! I gotta get you back to the White House so you can get him ready to sign the peace treaty with—"

VROOOM!!!!!!!

I didn't hear the rest of what she said because as soon as I got in the limo, she stomped on the gas and we went zooming through the city WAY TOO FAST!

"You know," said the Countess, "if you were a hip-hop star, you'd get to ride in a limo every day."

"I don't want to be a hip-hop star!" I shouted. "And I don't want to ride in a limo ever again! How can you possibly drive a car this long through the city this fast?"

"I can't," said the Countess. "In fact, we're about to crash into the Washington Monument."

We crashed into the Washington Monument.

As we stumbled out of the wrecked limo, Policedog Brenda zoomed up on a hoverboard.

"This is a no-parking zone!" she yelled.

"But this is the president's limo!" the Countess yelled back.

"Oh, sorry," said Policedog Brenda. "Go right ahead." She zoomed away.

Countess Zuzu Poodle-oo pointed to her map.

"See, the White House is just an easy walk from here."

Interlude

As we walked toward the White House, we passed a bunch of street vendors. They had little tables and carts set up to sell things.

There was an iguana selling hats that said PRESIDENT HORSE IS GREAT! She had no customers.

Next to her was a komodo dragon selling hats that said PRESIDENT HORSE IS *NOT* GREAT." He had a lot of customers.

"Why don't people want the 'is great' hats?" I asked the iguana.

"Ever since he declared war on Wingland, everyone is mad at him. Especially people from Wingland."

"Are you going to go out of business?"

"No, I'm just going to write 'NOT' on these hats with a Magic Marker," the iguana said.

The next street vendor we passed was a penguin selling meatball necklaces.

"Hello, Countess! Hello, DJ Funkyfoot!" the penguin called.

"Hello, Penguini!" I said. "I did not know you had a food cart. What happened to your rooftop restaurant?"

"I realized that I was afraid of heights!"

he said. "So now I have a street cart so I can cook my food at ground level. Speaking of food, have a free sample of my new  recipe: spaghetti and mulchballs!"

"Uh, no thank you," I said, trying hard to be polite. "I know my friend ShrubBaby would love that, but I . . . I should hurry into the White House and start my job as the president's butler."

"Tell the president he'd better sign the peace treaty with Wingland!" said Penguini. "I do not want a war with Wingland!"

"As a butler, it is not my job to tell the president what to do," I replied. "He will tell me what to do."

"HMMPH!" snorted Penguini.

PART 2

Back in the Saddle

Chapter 4

When we got to the White House, the Countess showed me where to go in, then she went to call a tow truck for the president's limo.

There were a lot of security guards at the White House. I had to explain why I was there to a gnu, a water buffalo, and a musk ox.

Finally, the musk ox took me to the president's office.

Before we went into the office, the musk ox looked at her watch.

"Make sure you have the president ready at eleven o'clock," said the musk ox. "He has to sign a peace treaty with Wingland."

"That sounds important," I said.

"It is!" she whispered. "If he doesn't sign it, the war will start at eleven thirty!"

Then she opened the door and I stepped inside.

It was a very fancy office, just like I had seen on the TV news many times.

Behind an enormous desk sat President Horse G. Horse himself.

"Good day, Mr. President," I said in my most butlery voice. "Would you like a cup of tea before you sign the peace treaty, sir?"

"Who the hoof are you?" yelled the president. "Someone call the air force! There's a small wolf in my office!"

"I am not a small wolf, Mr. President," I said. "I am DJ Funkyfoot, and I am your butler for today."

"I don't want you to be my butler!" he yelled, stomping his hoof on his desk. "Where's my other butler?"

"He's playing miniature golf today, sir," I replied very calmly, even though President Horse was shouting.

"Oh goody! I want to play miniature golf, too!" he yelled.

"I'm sorry, Mr. President, but you are supposed to get ready to sign a peace treaty with Wingland, sir."

"BUT I WANT TO PLAY MINI GOLF!!!!!"

he screamed, stomping all his hooves on his desk.

"Perhaps, sir, you might play mini golf after—" I began.

"NO! NO!! NO!!!" he neighed, throwing himself on the carpet and kicking his legs in the air. "NOW! NOW!! NOW!!!"

"But, sir, you—"

"MOMMY!!!!"

Chapter 5

A door opened and another horse galloped into the room. It was the president's mom.

"What's wrong, my sweet widdle baby president?"

"Mommy, you said being president would be fun, but it's no fun! I never get to do what I want to do!"

"Oh, you poor sweet widdle horsie, what is it you want to do?"

"I wanna play mini golf! But this wolf won't let me!"

The president's mom whirled around and glared at me. She pawed at the carpet with her hoof.

"How dare you?" she bellowed.

I was getting scared! But I remembered my butler training and tried to answer calmly.

"The musk ox told me that—"

"A musk ox told YOU? And who ARE you?"

"My name is DJ Funkyfoot, ma'am."

"DJ Funkyfoot? The butler?"

I could hardly believe that someone finally knew I was a butler and not a hip-hop star!

"Yes! How did—"

"You used to work for my good friend Countess Zuzu Poodle-oo. Is that correct?" she asked me, still bellowing and still angry.

"Yes, I—"

"And when you worked for Countess Poodle-oo, did you tell her what to do, or did she tell you what to do?"

"She told me—"

"So, why do you walk into the White House and think you can tell the President of the United States of America what to do?"

"I—"

"As his butler, isn't it your job to do what he tells you to do?"

She was right!

I had told Penguini that I would do what the president told me to do, but then I had done the opposite.

"Yes, ma'am. I beg your pardon, ma'am. I will now escort the President of the United States of America to play mini golf, ma'am."

"And let him win," she whispered in my ear.

Chapter 6

President Horse G. Horse was very happy now.

"I wanna go to the one that has the pirate ship and the waterfall and the mermaid that spits your ball into a hole!"

"Yes, Mr. President," I said. "Would you like to have a cup of tea first?"

"NO, I'll get a big pirate barrel full of red soda when we get there! Let's go! Let's go now!"

I could barely keep up with the president as he galloped out of his office, through the White House, and out the front door.

"WHERE'S MY LIMO???" he yelled.

"Uh," said Countess Zuzu Poodle-oo. "It's parked near the Washington Monument."

"I don't know where that is," said the president.

"Maybe I could—" began the Countess.

"There's no time for maybes!" the president yelled at her. "There's only time for pirate-themed mini golf. I'll just gallop over there myself."

The president put his front hooves on the ground.

"Hop on, GG Monkeyfoot!" he demanded.

"Uh . . ."

"NOW!"

The next-to-the-last thing I wanted to do was ride through the streets of Washington, DC, on the back of a galloping president.

But the very last thing I wanted to do was lose my job!

So I said, "Yes, sir, Mr. President," and jumped on his back.

"Giddyup, me!" he neighed.

Then he galloped across the White House lawn, leaped over the fence, and zigzagged through the busy streets.

"Outta my way!" he yelled at a kiwi driving a truck.

"National emergency!" he yelled at some pigs on a bus.

"So long, losers!" he yelled at everybody.

"Shouldn't you stop for this red light?" I asked.

"I'm the President of the United States," he said, "and I do what I want. And you are my butler, so you do what I want, too! Right?"

"Yes, sir, Mr. President," I said, clinging to his mane as he charged through the red light, right between two speeding Cousin Yuk Yuk's Pickle Relish trucks.

COUSIN
YUK YUK'S
PICKLE
RELISH

Interlude

was so happy when we stopped in front of a statue of a giant peg-leg pirate.

The statue was holding a big sign.

The sign said GIANT PEG-LEG PIRATE'S MINI GOLF AND FONDUE FUN SPOT!

"Oh boy," said President Horse. "I like fun! And I like pirates! And I like golf! But what is 'fon-du-wee'?"

"That is pronounced 'fon-do,' sir," I said. "It is fancy hot cheese dip."

"Oh boy!" yelled President Horse. "I love fancy hot cheese dip! That must be what's in the waterfall coming out of the volcano!"

"Hmm," I said, "all I see is a volcano shooting fake lava at a pirate ship."

"Not that volcano," snapped President Horse, waving a hoof wildly. "THAT volcano!"

I looked and saw that, yes, the other volcano had a cheese waterfall.

"Ah, now I see, sir. You mean the volcano looming over the castle that shoots golf balls out of catapults?"

"Of course that's what I mean!" shouted President Horse. "Stop asking me questions and go rent golf clubs and balls from the Giant Peg-Leg Pirate!"

I went over to a little booth. Inside, there was a pineapple dressed like a pirate. He was watching TV.

"May I speak to the Giant Peg-Leg Pirate?" I asked.

"He ain't here, matey," said the pineapple. "He's out looking for his lost shoe . . . again!"

"Well, maybe you can help me," I said. "I need to rent a golf club and a ball."

Without looking up from his TV, the pineapple handed me a club, a ball, and a tiny scoresheet.

"That'll be thirty-eight dollars, matey!"

As I got out my wallet, I asked him what he was watching on TV.

"The big peace ceremony is about to start!" he said. "The Queen of Wingland is already there. Now they're just waiting for President Horse G. Horse!"

"Uh-oh," I said.

"Don't worry," said the pineapple. "The war doesn't start for another hour. There's plenty of time to sign the peace treaty!"

"How long does it take to play eighteen holes of pirate-themed mini golf?" I asked.

"Oh, about an hour," said the pineapple.

"HURRY UP, ZB Funnyhoof!" the president yelled at me. "And don't forget my big barrel full of red soda!"

I hurried!

PART 3
....
Par for the Horse

Chapter 7

At the first hole, President Horse G. Horse spent five minutes lining up his shot and fiddling with his golf club.

Finally, he said, "Do you think I should bank my shot off the octopus or the squid?"

"The squid, sir, definitely the squid."

Actually, I didn't care, I just wanted him to get started.

The president took a huge swing and hit the ball way too hard! It bounced off the octopus and came right back and hit me in the head!

"OUCH!"

"You got what you deserved," said the president, sipping about a gallon of his red soda. "That was terrible advice."

"But . . . I told you to hit the squid," I groaned. I was so dizzy I forgot to say "sir" or "Mr. President."

"That's exactly what I did!"

"No, you hit the octopus . . . and the butler," I moaned.

"I did not! I hit the squid!"

"But—"

SLURRP

"Say that I hit the squid!"

"What?"

"You have to do what I want, and I want you to say I hit the squid! Remember, I am the president and you are my butler."

I remembered.

"Yes, sir, Mr. President, you hit the squid," I lied.

I do not like to lie. My mother raised me never to lie. Of course, she also raised me to be a hip-hop star. Things weren't working out the way she wanted. OR the way I wanted either.

But they were working out the way the president wanted.

"If I hadn't listened to you, that shot would have gone in," he said. "So just write 'hole in one' on the scorecard."

"Yes, sir," I said.

At least this meant we could go on to the second hole. We had already wasted ten minutes!

Chapter 8

At hole two we wasted another ten minutes!

The president kept hitting the ball, but he just couldn't get it to go into the alligator's mouth.

"DO-OVER!" he yelled every time.

Finally I got a chance to swish it in with my tail. Unfortunately, my tail got chomped, too!

"Another hole in one!" shouted the president. "Write it down!"

"Yes, sir, Mr. President," I said. And I did.

"And go get me another barrel of soda! This time with extra sugar!"

"Yes, sir, Mr. President," I said. And I did.

At hole three we wasted ANOTHER ten minutes!

This hole had a castle with a plastic dragon. The dragon kept moving back and forth in front of the hole. Every time the president hit the ball, the ball hit the dragon and bounced back.

"This isn't fair! There should be a law against this!" yelled the president. "In

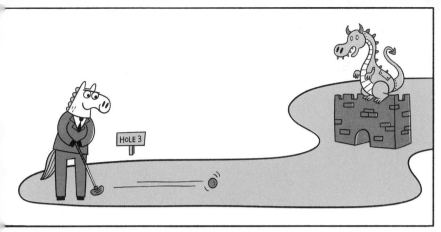

fact, since I'm the president, I just made a law, the No More Golf Dragon Law."

"Very good, sir," I said. "Shall we move on to the next hole?"

"NO, NO, NO! Not until I get a hole in one!" he yelled. "I am going to use my mighty horse strength to hit the ball so hard, it knocks the head off that illegal dragon!"

HOLE 3

Then the president used his mighty horse strength to hit the ball so hard that it bounced off the dragon and flew high into the air.

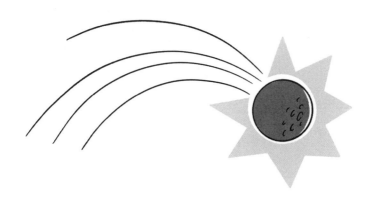

Chapter 9

J ust then the president's real butler, Cedric Dragonsmasher, showed up.

"Mr. President, what are you doing here?"

"DUCK!" I yelled.

"Duck?" replied Dragonsmasher. "You mean the duck who's the Queen of Wingland? What is she doing here? Also, you should have said 'Duck, sir.' After all—"

That's when the president's golf ball

came back down and hit Cedric Dragon-smasher on the head.

Cedric Dragonsmasher fell over, smashing the dragon.

The president's ball now bounced past the dragon, rolled through the castle, and went into the hole.

"Another hole in one!" shouted the president. "Write it down!"

"Yes, sir, Mr. President," I said. And I did.

I didn't like lying and helping him cheat, but there was no time to argue! The war was going to start in half an hour if I couldn't get him back to the White House to sign that peace treaty!

If he spent ten minutes on every hole . . . we were doomed!

I helped up Cedric Dragonsmasher.

"Now, can you help me, sir?" I asked.

"I'm sorry, sir, but it is my day off."

"But, sir, this is a national emergency!"
I pleaded.

"Sir," he replied, "every day is a national
emergency when President Horse is
around. That's why I needed a day off, sir!
Now, sir, if you'll excuse me, I'm going to
go finish my fondue."

"Please, sir," I said. "Just do one thing for me . . . Call the Queen of Wingland and tell her to come here and bring the peace treaty with her."

"Oh, hoober roofus!" he grumbled, pulling out his phone. "Fine, I'll call the queen, but then I am going to dip doughnuts in that hot cheese waterfall and nobody can stop me!"

A Train Bound for Narwhal

Chapter 10

S top talking to other animals and pay attention to me!" President Horse yelled at me.

"Yes, sir," I said.

"What's my score?"

I looked at the scorecard.

His real score was 359, but I lied. "Three, sir."

"Perfect!" he said. "I plan to get a perfect score on all eighteen holes!"

"Ahem, sir, there is not enough time for all eighteen holes. In fact, it's time to leave right now, sir."

"But I don't want to leave right now!" he screamed. "You can't do what I don't want because I don't want you to cannot do it when it's not what I want so you don't can't never not ever nope uh-uh I said no I'm the big boy my mom said so you're just a butler and can't not make me want to don't not go!!!!!!!!"

"But, sir!"

"NO!!!!!!" he yelled.

He took his golf ball and club to the next hole.

"Now I am going to hit this ball into the mermaid's belly button, and you are going to say, 'Very good, sir!'"

He hit the ball.

For once it was a good shot.

It was going right for the mermaid's belly button.

It was going to be a hole in one!

"I am sorry, sir," I said very calmly and politely, just like butlers are supposed to do. But then I did something that butlers are NOT supposed to do.

I put my foot down . . . in front of the mermaid's belly button.

The ball bounced off my foot and rolled into the hot cheese river.

The president stamped all of his hooves at once. He snorted. He whinnied. He shouted, "Hoober roofus." He shouted, "Meega weega dimpleham." And then he shouted, "You are a bad bad butler!"

He was right! I had been a bad butler. But that was OK, because I had just learned something important. You can't say yes to everything. Sometimes even a butler has to put his foot down.

"Mr. President, your golf game is over," I said. "It's time for you to sign that peace treaty!"

"Oh, yeah? Who's going to make me?"

"I am!"

"What's your name again? I forgot."

"DJ Funkyfoot!"

"Really? Are you a hip-hop star?"

"NO, I'M NOT!"

"Well, BJ Flunkyfool who's not a hip-hop star and also not a very good butler . . . you've got to catch me first!"

And he took off running!

So I did, too!

Chapter 11

The President of the United States of America jumped across the moat and galloped away through a diorama of King Arthur jousting with Joan of Arc.

I was too small to leap across the moat, so I had to wait for the drawbridge to come down. When it did, I raced across and ran between King Arthur's royal legs, which, I noticed, had termites.

By this time, President Horse had jumped on the tiny train that runs through the golf course.

"You'll never catch me now, FF Dunky-joot!" he yelled.

But luckily for me, the train crashed into a narwhal on the sixteenth hole.

CRASH!

President Horse G. Horse was thrown clear of the wreck, bounced off the nar-whal, and landed in a field of fake flowers next to a beautiful unicorn.

"Hey, baby," he said to the unicorn. "I'll be back later, and we can go on a date with lots of kissing."

"Mr. President! That's not even a real unicorn! Now, let's go sign the treaty!"

"Well, you're not even a real butler, PP Punkypoot, so I won't go sign the treaty."

He kissed the fake unicorn goodbye—its head fell off—and he jumped over the edge of a cliff and onto the big pirate ship in the center of the golf course.

It was too far for me to jump, but I was able to grab on to a flying Pegasus. Like the unicorn, it was fake, but it was filled with helium. Also like the unicorn, its head fell off, and all the helium hissed out.

I fell like a rock, right onto the big pirate ship.

"Time to go sign that treaty, sir," I said.

"I said I don't wanna!" he wailed, backing away.

"You must!"

"NUH-UH!" he neighed. He kept backing away until he had backed himself out onto the pirate's plank, which stretched out over the hot cheese volcano.

"There's no way out, Mr. President. So just come with me and sign the peace treaty!"

"NO! NO, NO, NO!" he yelled, stamping his hooves. "I'd rather fall into a hot cheese volcano than let somebody tell ME what to do!"

He took a step backward, fell off the end of the plank, and fell into the cheese volcano.

He disappeared under the cheese.

I was getting ready to dive in after him, when his head popped above the surface.

"Ha ha, I win!" he neighed. "This is really very nice. I could stay in here for hours!"

"But you've got to go sign that treaty!" I begged.

"Nope! Too busy sitting in cheese! It's kind of like a Jacuzzi!"

The pineapple came running out of his booth.

"Hey, get out of there! You're clogging up the cheese volcano!"

"No," said President Horse. "I'm the president. Nobody can tell me what to do. Not you. Not JD Footfunk. Not even the Queen of Wingland!"

I looked at my watch.

The war was going to start in five minutes.

I had failed at saving the world and I had failed at being a good butler. I'd never even gotten to make a cup of tea!

Chapter 12

HONK HONK! SCREECH! SMASH!

Countess Poodle-oo drove up in a tow truck. It was towing the president's limo.

The limo opened and a dodo wearing roller skates, a small zebra in a suit, and a duck got out.

"Thanks for the ride, Countess," said the dodo.

"Anytime, Didi," said the Countess.

Then a van full of TV news reporters pulled up.

Greta Von Hoppinstop jumped out with her TV camera.

"We're ready to film the signing, Your Royal Highness!" she yelled.

"And I am ready to sign," the duck, who was the Queen of Wingland, said. "How much time is left before the war starts?"

"Two and a half minutes, Your Royal Highness," said the zebra.

"WELL?" the queen demanded. "Where is the President of the United States of America?"

"I beg your pardon, Your Royal Highness," I said. "He is in the cheese volcano, Your Royal Highness."

"Cheese volcano?

All I see is a regular volcano shooting fake lava at a pirate ship."

"I meant the other volcano, Your Royal Highness," I said. "The one that is currently rumbling, grumbling, and making strange noises."

"Why is it rumbling, grumbling, and making strange noises?" asked the queen.

Just then the pineapple came running out of his tiny booth again.

"It's gonna blow!!!!!"

"Hey!" yelled the zebra. "You're talking to the queen!"

"Sorry!" yelled the pineapple, bowing. "It's the cheese volcano, Your Royal Highness! Something has stopped up the cheese sauce, Your Royal Highness! The pressure is building, Your Royal Highness!"

"In other words," said the queen, "IT'S GONNA BLOW!!!!!"

It BLEW.

Epilogue

President Horse landed in the middle of us with a big, cheesy splash!

The dodo and the zebra jumped to protect the queen from the hot cheese.

As he jumped, the zebra dropped the peace treaty.

It fell on the ground.

President Horse G. Horse staggered to his feet. His head was so covered in cheese that he couldn't see where he was stepping.

 With one cheesy hoof he stomped on the peace treaty.

It left behind a big cheesy hoofprint.

The queen dipped one of her webbed feet in cheese and made her own footprint.

"THE TREATY IS SIGNED!" yelled the zebra. "WITH ELEVEN SECONDS TO SPARE!"

"There will be no war!" the news reporters yelled into their cameras. "There's peace on Earth!"

"How did this happen?" asked Greta Von Hoppinstop. "Who stopped the war?"

"The butler did it!" groaned President Horse. Then he got in his limo and the

Countess towed him back to the White House.

I was busy the rest of the day telling reporters that I was a butler and not a hip-hop star, so I really don't know how he got all of that cheese sauce out of his mane.

I know I wasn't the world's best butler today, but . . . like I said, sometimes even a butler has to put his foot down.

Dive into another case in

DJ Funkyfoot #3:
The Show Must Go Oink

Opening

My phone rang.

"Greetings," I said. "I am DJ Funkyfoot and I am at YOUR service."

"Hello, DJ Funkyfoot," said a cool voice. "I am Krystal Wombat, president of Wombat Jam Records."

I was very excited!

Company presidents are often rich.

And rich people can hire butlers.

And I am a butler!

Since butlers are always very polite, I answered Krystal Wombat as politely as I possibly could.

"Madame Wombat," I said. "It would be my great honor to serve as your butler!"

"Oh, I've already got a butler," she said. "What I need is a hot hip-hop hit record. That's why I'm calling you."

ALAS! This was yet another phone call from someone who thought I was a hip-hop star because of my name, DJ Funky-foot. (Middle name: MC.)

My parents hoped that I would become a hip-hop star. They gave me this name. They made me take hip-hop lessons. They bought me turntables and microphones.

But through it all, I followed a different dream.

The dream of being a butler! Of serving fancy tea and fancy food on fancy dishes in a very fancy way.

Unfortunately, every time someone hires me to be a butler, things don't turn out fancy. They turn out messy—very messy—and I lose the job.

"Well," said Krystal Wombat, with a voice that was a little less cool and a little more impatient. "Do you have a hot hip-hop hit record? Your mother told me you did!"

"My mother?"

"Yes, I ran into her at Cousin Yuk Yuk's Pickle Buffet, and she told me to call you to hear your latest, hottest, hip-hoppest recording."

"I am sorry," I said. "My mom was just bragging. I do not have a recording to play for you."

"I understand," she said. "Moms do that sometimes. But let me know if you ever do have a record to play for me."

"Yes, Madame Wombat," I said. "I certainly will."

PART 1

This Is a Job for Job for Super Butler!

Chapter 1

My phone rang again!

"Greetings," I said. "I am DJ Funkyfoot, and I am—"

Before I could finish, a very deep but very fancy voice grunted at me.

"No, I do not need a DJ. I need a butler. Goodbye."

"Wait!" I shouted. And then I remembered that butlers don't shout. So I said very politely, "Sir, I AM a butler."

VERY BEST
BUTLER

"Are you sure?" grunted the very deep but very fancy voice. "To me you sound like a hip-hop star who shouts."

"No, sir," I said. "I am indeed a butler, and I am at your service."

"Hurmmmmmmm," grunted the voice thoughtfully.

Then there was a long awkward pause. Should I say something else? Or should I give him time to think? I was excited about possibly getting a job as a butler, BUT a butler should not get too excited. So I decided to wait.

Finally the voice grunted again.

"I don't need just any butler. I need a butler who can do things EXACTLY the way that I ask. I need the very best butler. Are you the very best butler?"

I thought about my career as a butler so far—the disasters, the messes, the car wrecks. Could I really claim to be the "best" butler? No. But if I didn't claim to be the best butler, I wouldn't get the job. I said the only thing I could.

"I TRY to be the best butler, sir," I said. "And I will TRY to do everything exactly the way you ask."

"EXACTLY?" squealed the voice, which suddenly got very high-pitched.

"Exactly, sir," I said.

"All right. You are hired," grunted the voice, suddenly very low again. "You must be ready at once! We leave the city in one hour for the HooberHustle Music Festival!"

"You have a ticket for the Hoober-Hustle Music Festival? I thought it sold out in seconds!" I said. I was so surprised that I forgot to talk like a butler for a second. I hoped my new grunting boss was not annoyed.

He *was* annoyed, but not about that.

"No, I do not have a ticket!" he grunted very deep, very fancy, and very annoyed. "I will not be in the audience! I will be on the stage! For I am THE GREAT WOLFGOOSE PIGWIG, the STAR of the music festival!"

The adventure continues in

DJ Funkyfoot #3:
The Show Must Go Oink

Collect all of
THE FLYTRAP FILES

ABOUT THE AUTHOR AND ILLUSTRATOR

TOM ANGLEBERGER is the *New York Times* bestselling author of the Origami Yoda series, as well as many other books for kids. He created DJ Funkyfoot, a Chihuahua butler, with his wife, Cece Bell, for the Inspector Flytrap series. In real life, Tom and Cece do have a Chihuahua, but he's more of a biter than a butler. Visit Tom at origamiyoda.com.

HEATHER FOX is an illustrator of stories for children. When she isn't creating, she's probably drinking a hot cup of coffee, eating Chinese food, or chasing down her dog, Sir Hugo, who has stolen one of her socks. She lives in Lancaster, Pennsylvania, with her husband (and author!) Jonathan Stutzman.